P. Crumble and Jonathan Bentley

WE ARE ALL EQUAL

PHILOMEL BOOKS

WE ARE ALL EQUAL

Your day's not like mine.

I chew on bamboo,

you swing on a vine.

WE ARE ALL EQUAL

You've crossed land and sea.

This country's your home now,

it's for you and me.

WE ARE ALL EQUAL

Our kids we adore.

Just 'cause we're parents,
we aren't worth more.

WE ARE ALL EQUAL

Your house may be small.

I am not better

with room to stand tall.

WE ARE ALL EQUAL

You can't walk or run.

It doesn't take legs

to have lots of fun.

WE ARE ALL EQUAL

You're shaped unlike me.

I'm small and slender,
you're strong and sturdy.

We Are All Equal

Our love we decide.

We can get married,

no love is denied.

WE ARE ALL EQUAL

You're kind and carefree.

Beauty is deeper
than what you can see.

We Are All Equal

While you're not as strong,

bullying isn't

the way to belong.

We ARE ALL EQUAL

If only you knew,

tests cannot measure

the good you will do.

WE ARE ALL EQUAL

Let's shout it out loud.

We share hopes and dreams.
We're equal and proud.

To all those who take steps each day to create a more equal world —PC

For Clive and Neil —JB

Philomel Books
An imprint of Penguin Random House LLC, New York

First published in the United States of America by Philomel Books,
an imprint of Penguin Random House LLC, 2020.

First published in Australia by Scholastic Australia in 2018.

Visit us online at penguinrandomhouse.com

Library of Congress Cataloging-in-Publication Data is available.

Manufactured in China.

ISBN 9780593202555

10 9 8 7 6 5 4 3 2 1

Edited by Talia Benamy. Design by Ellice Lee. Text set in 23 pt. Austral Slab.